A catalogue record for this book is available from the British Library

Published by Ladybird Books Ltd Loughborough Leicestershire UK
Ladybird Books Ltd is a subsidiary of the Penguin Group of companies
LADYBIRD and the device of a Ladybird are trademarks of Ladybird Books Ltd

Printed in Belgium

Beauty and the Beast

Ladybird

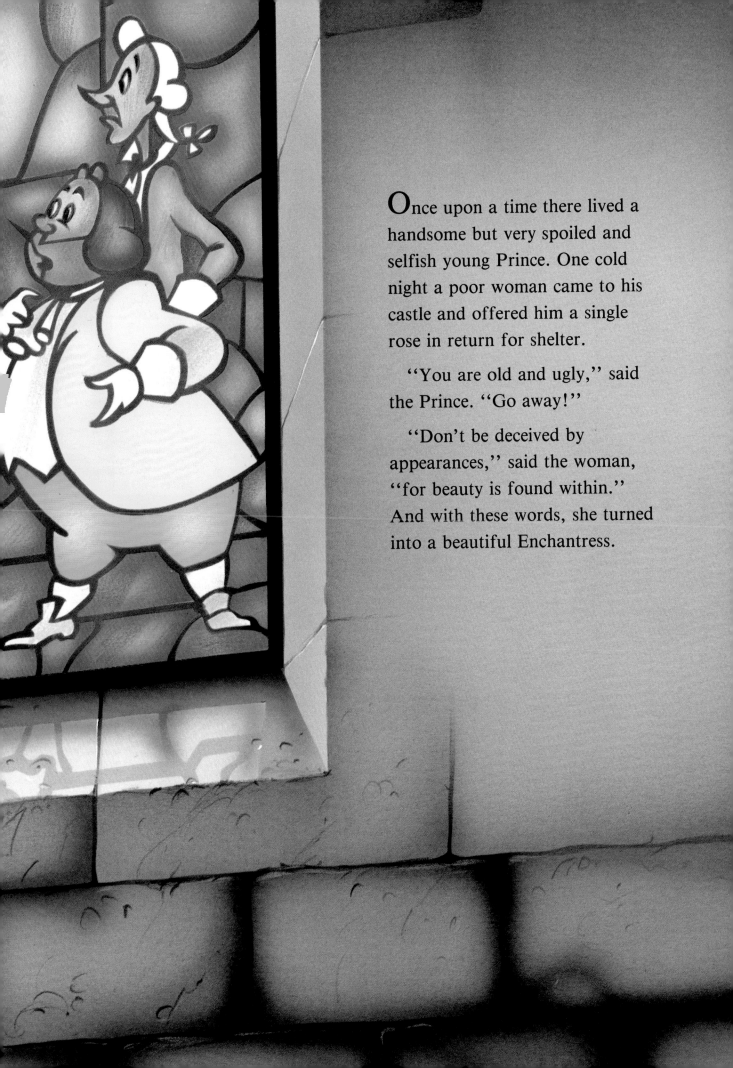

Once upon a time there lived a handsome but very spoiled and selfish young Prince. One cold night a poor woman came to his castle and offered him a single rose in return for shelter.

"You are old and ugly," said the Prince. "Go away!"

"Don't be deceived by appearances," said the woman, "for beauty is found within." And with these words, she turned into a beautiful Enchantress.

To punish the Prince for his unkindness, the Enchantress transformed him into a hideous Beast, and cast a spell on everyone in the castle.

She left the Prince a magic mirror and the rose he had refused to accept. It was an enchanted rose that would bloom until his twenty-first year. If the Prince could learn to love and earn another person's love in return before the last petal of the rose fell, the spell would be broken. If not, he would remain a beast for ever.

Not far from the castle was a little village, where a beautiful young girl named Belle lived. Because she always had her nose in a book, the villagers thought Belle was a bit strange. Still, they were fond of her, for she was kind and gentle.

One autumn morning, as Belle crossed the town square, Gaston, the most handsome man in the village, passed by. Gaston was also the most conceited man in the village, and when he saw Belle he thought, "She's the only girl beautiful enough to be worthy of me. I'm going to marry her!"

Just then Belle heard a loud explosion from her cottage. "Papa!" she cried, running for home.

Luckily Belle's father, Maurice, was all right. But his latest invention was not. The jumbled collection of pipes, pulleys, wheels and levers spluttered and spewed smoke.

"I'll never get this thing to work!" said Maurice. "I'm supposed to show it at the fair tomorrow!"

"Don't worry, Papa," said Belle soothingly. "You *will* get it to work."

Inspired by Belle's confidence in him, Maurice picked up his tools and went back to work. And later that afternoon, he and his faithful horse, Philippe, set off with the invention for the fair.

15

As Maurice and Philippe travelled through the woods, a thick fog enveloped them. Soon they were lost.

Then, through the mist, they heard the menacing snarls of wolves. Suddenly a blood-curdling howl pierced the air, and Philippe reared up in alarm, throwing Maurice to the ground. Terror-stricken, Philippe fled.

Maurice staggered through the forest, desperate to escape from the wolves. When he found himself in front of a gloomy, neglected castle, he wrenched open the rusty gate and rushed inside.

"Hello?" called Maurice, stepping inside a huge, empty hall.

"Not a word!" whispered a clock to a golden candelabra.

"Oh, Cogsworth, have a heart," said Lumiere, the candelabra. "The poor man must have lost his way in the woods. You are welcome here, Monsieur!" he called out.

Maurice was stunned. He seemed to be surrounded by enchanted objects!

21

Cogsworth was nervous. The Master would be furious! Guests were *never* allowed at the castle! But Mrs Potts, the teapot, and her son, Chip, insisted that Maurice should warm himself by the fire.

All at once the Beast stormed into the room. The enchanted objects scuttled away, fearing their Master's rage. "A stranger!" roared the Beast. "Strangers are not welcome here!" He grabbed Maurice in his powerful claws and carried him off to a dark, cold dungeon.

23

The next morning, as Belle awaited her father's return, Gaston came to see her. Belle reluctantly let him in, not realising that he had come to propose to her – and marry her right then and there! A crowd of villagers had come to watch.

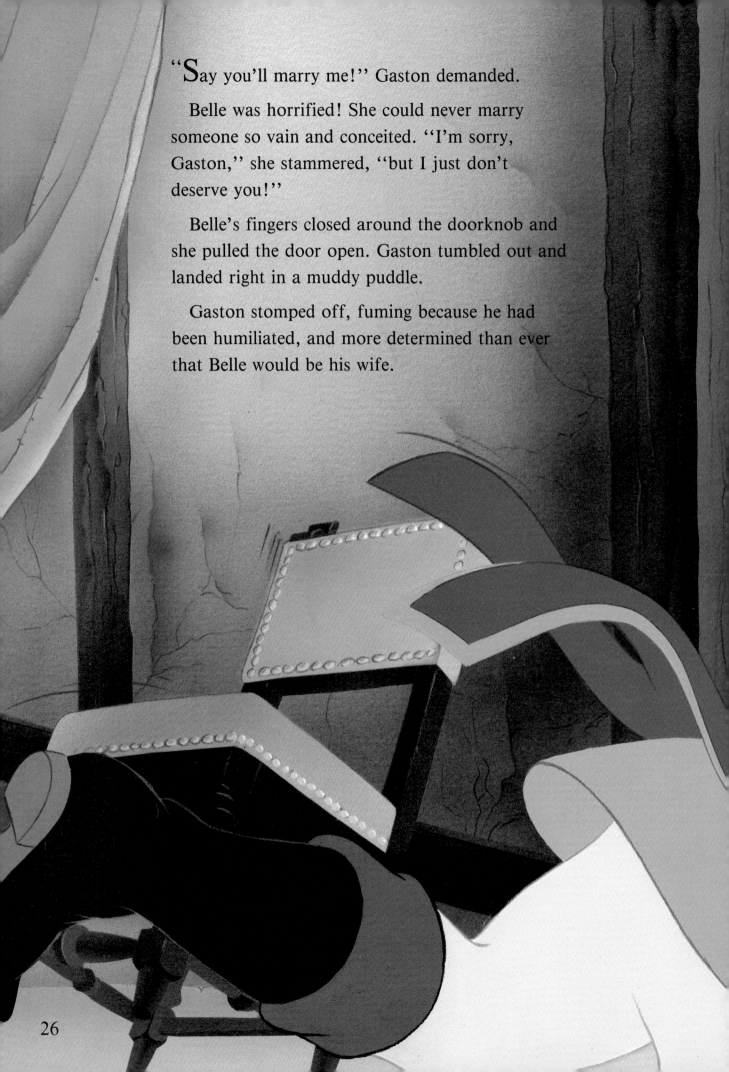

"Say you'll marry me!" Gaston demanded.

Belle was horrified! She could never marry someone so vain and conceited. "I'm sorry, Gaston," she stammered, "but I just don't deserve you!"

Belle's fingers closed around the doorknob and she pulled the door open. Gaston tumbled out and landed right in a muddy puddle.

Gaston stomped off, fuming because he had been humiliated, and more determined than ever that Belle would be his wife.

A short time later, when Belle was feeding the chickens, she heard Philippe's whinny. She turned to welcome her father, and was shocked to see that Philippe was alone!

"Philippe, where's Papa?" she cried. The horse just snorted anxiously and stamped the ground.

"Something's happened!" said Belle. "Oh, Philippe, you must take me to Papa!"

She leapt onto Philippe's back, and the horse carried her towards the dark forest.

Before long they were at the huge, forbidding castle. Belle pulled open the rusty gate, just as her father had, and went inside. Wandering through the gloomy halls, she called, "Papa? Are you here?" Cogsworth, Lumiere and Mrs Potts followed her quietly.

"She must be the one!" Lumiere whispered to the others. "She's the one who will break the spell!"

At last Belle found her father, frightened and freezing in his tiny cell.

"Oh, Papa!" she exclaimed. "We've got to get you out of here!"

All at once Belle sensed danger. She whirled around, just catching sight of a massive shape hiding in the shadows.

"What are you doing in my castle?" the Beast bellowed.

"I've come for my father," said Belle. "Please let him go. He's ill."

"He shouldn't have trespassed," said the Beast. "He's my prisoner now."

"Take me instead!" said Belle bravely.

The Beast hardly dared to believe what he was hearing. "Your father can go," he told Belle. "But you must stay here for ever."

Belle was curious to see whom she was talking to. "Come into the light," she said. The Beast took a deep breath and stepped out of the shadows. Belle gasped in horror, but she would not change her mind. "You have my word," she promised.

"Belle, no!" cried Maurice. "I won't let you do this!"

But the Beast dragged him from his cell and sent him home. Belle watched from the window, sobbing.

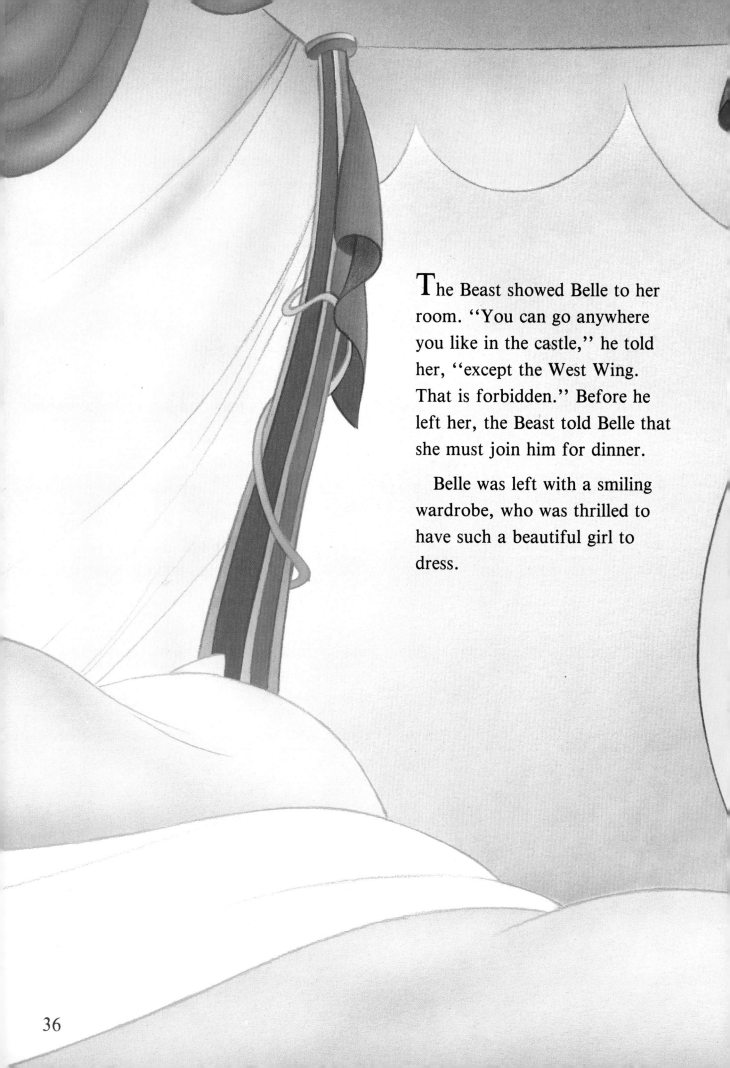

The Beast showed Belle to her room. "You can go anywhere you like in the castle," he told her, "except the West Wing. That is forbidden." Before he left her, the Beast told Belle that she must join him for dinner.

Belle was left with a smiling wardrobe, who was thrilled to have such a beautiful girl to dress.

37

"What would you like to wear to dinner?" said the Wardrobe cheerfully. She flung open her doors.

"It's kind of you to ask," said Belle, "but I'm not going to dinner."

"Oh, but you must!" cried the Wardrobe anxiously. Just then, Cogsworth appeared to announce importantly, "Dinner is served!"

When Cogsworth told him that Belle had refused to come to dinner, the Beast was furious. "She must obey my orders!" he roared. "If she doesn't eat with me, she doesn't eat at all!"

Back at the village tavern, Gaston was brooding about Belle when Maurice burst in, wild-eyed.

"Help, please!" he cried. "A monstrous beast is holding Belle prisoner. Someone must help me rescue her!"

Gaston and the others burst out laughing, convinced that the old inventor was crazy.

As Maurice was hustled out the door, Gaston pulled his friend Lefou aside. "That loony old man has just given me an idea!" he said.

Outside the tavern Maurice stood in a swirling mass of snow. "I'll have to rescue Belle on my own," he said despairingly.

43

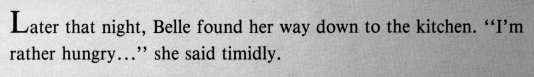

Later that night, Belle found her way down to the kitchen. "I'm rather hungry…" she said timidly.

"You are?" said Mrs Potts. "In that case, you shall have your dinner!"

"But the Master said she wasn't to eat!" protested Cogsworth.

"Nonsense!" said Mrs Potts, leading Belle to the dining room.

Under Lumiere's direction, the crockery and cutlery staged a splendid show for Belle, and the serving pieces brought in one delicious dish after another. Belle was delighted.

When the show was over, Belle stood up and cheered. "And now," she said, "may I look round the castle?"

"Of course!" said Lumiere. "We'll give you a tour!"

Belle knew she wasn't allowed in the West Wing, but she was terribly curious about it. When no one was looking, she managed to sneak upstairs.

She was shocked when she came upon the Beast's lair. It was dark and dirty, and strewn with broken furniture, torn clothes and cracked mirrors. The only beautiful thing in the room was the enchanted rose, glowing inside a glass jar. Entranced, Belle reached out to touch it.

Suddenly the Beast leapt in through the window. "Get out!" he roared. *"Get out!"*

Terrified, Belle raced down the stairs and fled from the castle. She climbed on Philippe's back, and together they escaped into the freezing night.

They hadn't got far when they heard growls and saw cruel yellow eyes gleaming in the dark. The wolves! Philippe broke into a gallop. Close behind him, the wolves snapped at his heels, and the frightened horse reared. Belle was flung to the ground.

Belle tried to defend herself and Philippe, but
the wolves were all around them. Belle stumbled
and fell, and a wolf, seeing its chance, went
straight for her throat.

All at once a huge paw snatched the wolf away.
The Beast had come to save her!

There was a fierce, violent
fight, but the wolves were no
match for the Beast. Realising
that they were beaten, they
whined and slunk away.

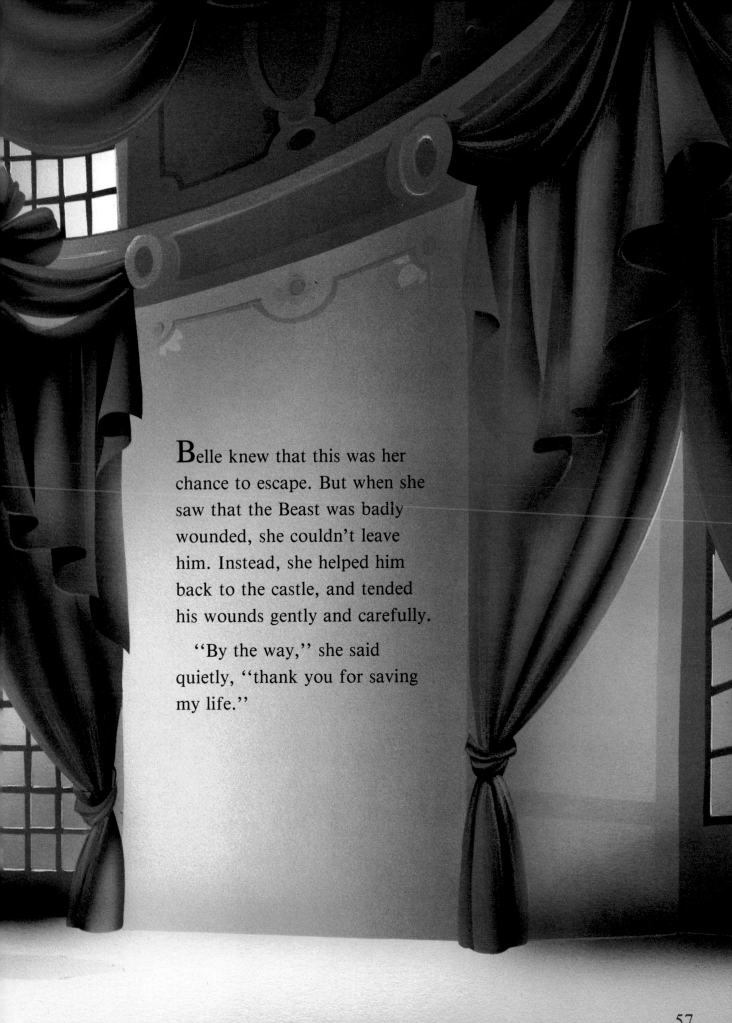

Belle knew that this was her
chance to escape. But when she
saw that the Beast was badly
wounded, she couldn't leave
him. Instead, she helped him
back to the castle, and tended
his wounds gently and carefully.

"By the way," she said
quietly, "thank you for saving
my life."

From that day on, a friendship grew between Belle and the Beast. Everyone in the household was thrilled to see what was happening.

The Beast showed Belle his enormous library. "All these books are yours, if you want them," he told her. Belle was happy to have dinner with the Beast now. She even tried to teach him table manners!

59

And one evening, after dinner, the Beast shyly led Belle into the ballroom, where they danced together to a beautiful love song. Then they went out onto the terrace.

"Belle," said the Beast, "are you happy here, with me?"

"Yes," said Belle. "But I miss my father. I wish I could see him."

"There is a way," said the Beast. He brought out the magic mirror. "This will show you anything you want to see," he explained.

Belle looked into the mirror – and saw Maurice lost in the forest, trembling with cold. "Belle," he called weakly. "Where are you?"

"Oh, no!" Belle cried. "Papa is ill! And he's all alone!"

"Then you must go to him," said the Beast. "But take the mirror, so you can look back – and remember me."

"Thank you for understanding how much he needs me," said Belle, touching the Beast's paw. Then she ran to the courtyard and rode away, as the Beast watched from the balcony.

"How could you let her go?" Cogsworth asked the Beast. "She was your last chance."

"I had to," said the Beast sadly, "because I love her."

With the mirror's help, Belle found Maurice and brought him home, where she soon nursed him back to health.

"I can't believe that horrible Beast let you go," said Maurice one day.

"He's different now, Papa," said Belle. "He's changed somehow."

Just then there was a knock at the door.

Belle answered it to find Gaston there with a crowd of villagers – and the director of the Insane Asylum!

"We've come to collect your father," he said.

"My father's not crazy," replied Belle angrily.

"He was raving about a monstrous beast," said Lefou. He knew that Gaston planned to have Maurice locked up unless Belle agreed to marry him.

"My father's not crazy!" shouted Belle. "I can prove it!"

Belle ran inside and got the mirror. "Show me the Beast!" she said.

When the villagers saw the Beast in the mirror, they screamed with terror. Furious that his plan hadn't worked, Gaston snatched the mirror away from Belle. "This Beast will make off with your children!" he warned the villagers. "He's a danger to us all! Who will come with me to kill him?"

Shouts of "We're with you, Gaston!" and "Kill the Beast!" rose from the crowd. Quickly, the villagers ran home to gather weapons and torches.

Guided by the mirror, Gaston led the angry mob through the forest to the Beast's castle.

Cogsworth, Lumiere and Mrs Potts saw the attackers approaching. "Invaders!" shouted Cogsworth. "Warn the Master!" He and the others scattered to rouse the rest of the household.

When the villagers broke into the castle, they were met by a host of angry enchanted objects ready to do battle. Thunder cracked the air and rain whipped out of the sky as the fighting began.

But up in his room, the Beast sat alone in despair. Now that Belle was gone, he didn't care what happened to his castle – or to him.

As the fighting raged below, Gaston found the Beast and forced him onto the battlements.

Belle and Maurice, who had been speeding towards the castle, arrived just in time to see Gaston beat the unresisting Beast and drive him towards the edge of the roof.

"No!" cried Belle. "Stop!" In desperation, she rode Philippe straight into the castle and up the stairs.

As soon as he heard Belle's voice, the Beast came to life. He gathered his strength and grabbed Gaston by the throat.

"Let me go!" begged Gaston. "Please! I'll do anything!"

The Beast could have finished Gaston then and there, but he had become too human to kill. Growling, he pushed Gaston aside and turned to Belle.

As the Beast reached out to embrace Belle, Gaston drew his dagger and plunged it into the Beast's back.

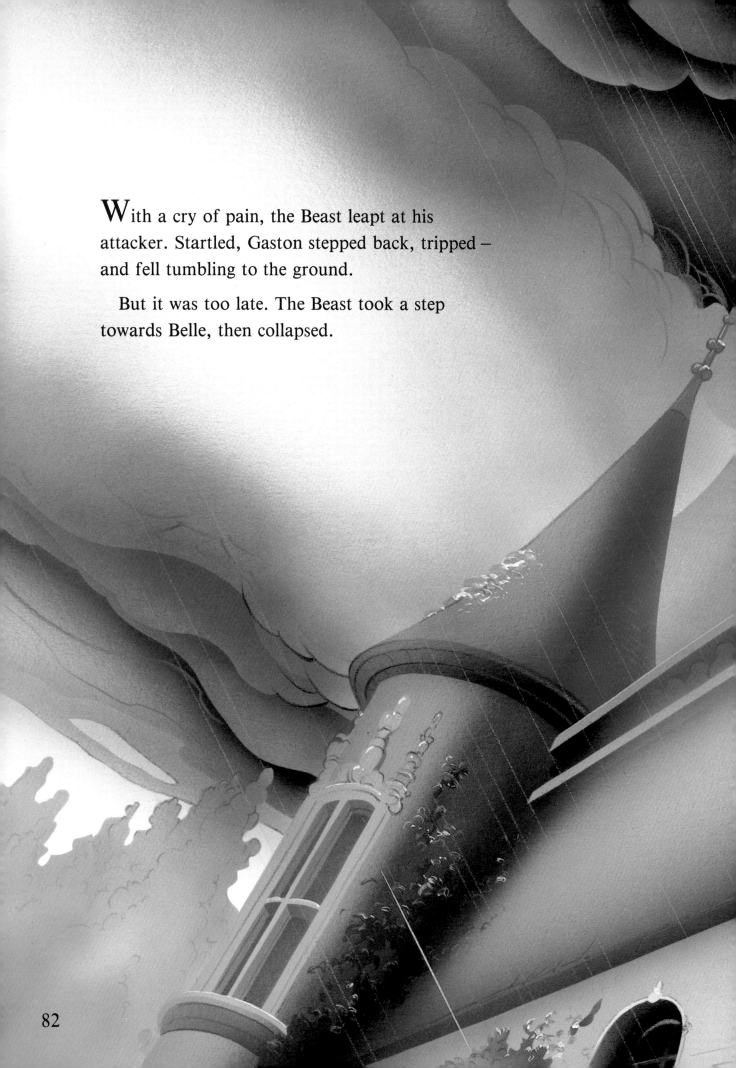

With a cry of pain, the Beast leapt at his attacker. Startled, Gaston stepped back, tripped — and fell tumbling to the ground.

But it was too late. The Beast took a step towards Belle, then collapsed.

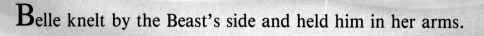

Belle knelt by the Beast's side and held him in her arms.

"You came back," he gasped. "At least I got to see you one last time."

"You'll be all right," said Belle, her voice choked with tears. In the Beast's room, the rose's last petal was about to fall.

"It's better this way," said the Beast, struggling for breath.

"NO!" sobbed Belle, leaning down to kiss him. "I love you!"

All at once, the raindrops began to shimmer and sparkle. The Beast blinked and looked around in amazement. His paw had become a human hand, and when he touched his face, it was smooth.

The spell was broken! The Beast had been transformed back into the Prince. In the tower, the dying rose burst into full bloom.

Belle couldn't understand what was happening, until the Prince said, "Belle... it's me."

As bright sunlight broke through the mist that had surrounded the castle for so long, the magic carried Belle and the Prince into the ballroom. They began to dance, and Cogsworth, Lumiere and Mrs Potts smiled as they watched. The magic swirled around them too, and they became the cheerful, friendly servants they had been before the spell.

Belle and the Prince could not stop looking at one another. Their eyes, and their hearts, were filled with wonder and love – the love that had broken the spell and brought them happiness for ever.